www.mascotbooks.com

For more information, please contact:
Mascot Books
560 Herndon Parkway #120
Herndon, VA 20170
info@mascotbooks.com

CPSIA Code: PRT1113A
ISBN-10: 1620864754
ISBN-13: 9781620864753

Printed in the United States

Hello, TC Bear!™

Naren Aryal
Illustrated by **Danny Moore**

It was a beautiful day in the Twin Cities of Minnesota. TC BEAR
was on his way to the ballpark for a baseball game.

As he walked through the city,
Twins fans cheered, "Hello, TC BEAR!"

The mascot was so excited to be going to the game,
and couldn't wait to watch his favorite team play.

In front of the ballpark, he ran into lots of
Twins fans. They cheered, "Hello, TC BEAR!"

TC BEAR arrived on the field just in time for batting practice.
Each player took swings to get ready for the game.

As the team's best hitter stepped to home plate,
he said, "Hello, TC BEAR!"

After batting practice, the grounds crew
proudly prepared the field for play.

As the grounds crew worked,
they hollered, "Hello, TC BEAR!"

TC BEAR was feeling hungry. He grabbed a few snacks and a *Twins* pennant at the concession stand.

As he made his way back to the field,
a family shouted, "Hello, TC BEAR!"

Each *Twins* player stood on the first base line
as the home team was introduced.

TC BEAR received the largest applause!
Fans roared, "Hello, TC BEAR!"

"PLAY BALL!" yelled the umpire. The *Twins'* pitcher delivered a
fastball to start the game. "STRIKE ONE!" called the umpire.

The umpire noticed the mascot nearby
and said, "Hello, TC BEAR!"

TC BEAR went into the bleachers to visit his fans.
Everyone was excited to see him.

A family waved and called out, "Hello, TC BEAR!"

It was now time for the seventh inning stretch. The mascot led
the crowd as everyone sang "Take Me Out To The Ballgame™!"

Young *Twins* fans danced on the dugout with TC BEAR.
They cheered, "Let's go, *Twins!*"

In the bottom of the ninth inning, a *Twins* player hit
a game-winning home run over the right-field fence.

The team gathered at home plate to celebrate the victory.
The players chanted, "*Twins* win, *Twins* win!"

After the game, TC BEAR was tired. It had been a long day at the ballpark. He walked home and went straight to bed.

Goodnight, TC BEAR!